The
Thanksgiving Surprise

Hmm, Nancy thought. Hannah didn't lose her ring at the grocery store or leave it lying around the house. She left it in the kitchen—and someone stole it!

Nancy hurried home. The sun was still shining brightly as she opened her front door.

"I'm home," Nancy called as she went to the coat closet.

No one answered.

"Is anyone here?" she called as she put her hand on the closet doorknob.

But before she could pull it open, it flew open! And something large leaped out at her!

The Nancy Drew Notebooks

Available from MINSTREL Books

THE
NANCY DREW
NOTEBOOKS™

#9

THE
THANKSGIVING SURPRISE

CAROLYN KEENE

Illustrated by Anthony Accardo

A MINSTREL® BOOK

PUBLISHED BY POCKET BOOKS

New York   London   Toronto   Sydney   Tokyo   Singapore

This book is a work of fiction. Names, characters, places and incidents are products of the author's imagination or are used fictitiously. Any resemblance to actual events or locales or persons, living or dead, is entirely coincidental.

A MINSTREL PAPERBACK *ORIGINAL*

A Minstrel Book published by
POCKET BOOKS, a division of Simon & Schuster Inc.
1230 Avenue of the Americas, New York, NY 10020

Copyright © 1995 by Simon & Schuster Inc.
Produced by Mega-Books, Inc.

ISBN: 0-671-52707-X

First Minstrel Books printing November 1995

10 9 8 7 6 5 4 3 2 1

NANCY DREW, A MINSTREL BOOK and colophon are registered trademarks of Simon & Schuster Inc.

THE NANCY DREW NOTEBOOKS is a trademark of Simon & Schuster Inc.

Cover art by Aleta Jenks

Printed in the U.S.A.

1

Thanksgiving Visitors

She hates me," Nancy Drew said. She was walking home from school with her best friend Bess Marvin. "Totally hates me."

"How can she hate you?" Bess asked. "She just met you."

"I know, but she does," Nancy said. "She'll hate you, too. Just wait and see. She hates everything here."

"That's not fair," Bess said, shaking her long blond hair.

It *isn't* fair, Nancy thought. But it was true. Pamela Morgan was from England. She and her family were visiting

Nancy's family. Her parents, Charles and Julie Morgan, were friends of Nancy's father. Nancy liked them. She liked their son, Derrick, too.

But Nancy didn't like Pamela one bit.

"She's so snooty," Nancy said. "She made fun of our cereal this morning—just because it wasn't oatmeal. And she asked for a cup of hot tea. For breakfast!"

Nancy pulled her jacket more tightly around her. She tucked her long reddish blond hair inside the collar.

It was a cold November day—the day before Thanksgiving. School had let out early. The sun was shining, but the air was cold.

Usually Nancy and Bess walked part of the way home with George Fayne. She was Bess's cousin and Nancy's other best friend. But George had gone away to visit relatives for Thanksgiving.

Nancy slowed down as she neared her house.

"There she is," Nancy said, lowering

her voice. She nodded toward a girl who was playing hopscotch in the driveway.

"Hmph," Bess said. "What's her name again?"

"Pamela," Nancy said. "Pamela Morgan."

"And she's going to make cookies with us?" Bess asked.

"Yes," Nancy said. "And so is her brother, Derrick."

Just as Nancy and Bess reached the driveway, the girl looked up. She was eight years old—Nancy's age. She had long brown hair, pink cheeks, and big blue eyes. Her navy blue wool coat had gold buttons down the front. It looked too fancy to wear for playing outside.

"Hi," Nancy said halfheartedly. "Pamela, this is my best friend Bess."

"Hello. Ever so nice to meet you," Pamela said in her crisp British accent.

"Hi," Bess said, shivering. "Nice to meet you, too. But aren't you cold? Let's go inside."

"We're supposed to play out here,"

Pamela said. "Your nanny just sent me out."

"My nanny? Who's that?" Nancy said. Then she realized. Pamela meant Hannah Gruen. Hannah was the Drew family's housekeeper. She had lived with the Drews and taken care of Nancy ever since Nancy's mother died.

"Oh, you mean Hannah," Nancy said.

"Yes," Pamela said. "And her friend, too. The one who's baking the pie."

Who could that be? Nancy wondered.

"The house is full of people," Pamela said.

"We'll be right back," Nancy said. She and Bess hurried in through the back door.

In the kitchen, Nancy saw what Pamela meant. Hannah and her friend Ann D'Angelo were there. Ann was talking to Hannah.

Ann's two children were sitting at the kitchen table. Ten-year-old Shelley was eating a peanut butter sandwich. Her dark hair was cut short, like her mother's. Her eyes were brown like her mother's, too. Her charm bracelets jangled as she ate. She had two bracelets on each arm.

Shelley's older brother, Greg, was eating grapes. Greg had brown hair and blue eyes. He was eleven years old—the same age as Pamela's brother, Derrick.

Derrick was standing behind Greg. He had thick copper-colored hair, a big smile, and twinkling brown eyes. He kept stealing grapes from Greg's plate when Greg wasn't looking.

"Don't take off your coats," Hannah said quickly when she saw Nancy and Bess. "I want you all to go play outside."

"But I thought we were going to make cookies," Nancy said.

"You will—but later," Hannah said. She put on her coat. "Right now I have to do some grocery shopping."

"Now?" Nancy asked.

"Yes," Hannah said. "We need fresh thyme and more apples for the turkey stuffing. Your father is out with the

Morgans, so Ann is going to stay here and take care of all of you."

"And bake a pumpkin pie," Ann said.

Hannah gave Ann a grateful smile.

"Now, go on outside—all of you," Ann ordered them. Then she began to mix the pumpkin and spices together.

Nancy gave Bess a disappointed look. She had really been looking forward to making cookies. She had a special turkey-shaped cookie cutter she wanted to use.

"But we haven't even had lunch yet," Nancy complained.

"Oh, that's right!" Hannah said. "Okay—make yourselves some peanut butter sandwiches, and *then* go out. I've got to hurry. The stores will be crowded."

Nancy and Bess put down their book bags and made lunch. Meanwhile, Shelley, Greg, and Derrick went outside.

When Nancy and Bess had finished eating, they went out to join the others.

"We're playing hide-and-seek," Derrick announced. His eyes twinkled.

"And you're it!" He tagged Nancy quickly.

Nancy laughed. "Okay," she said. She covered her eyes and counted to twenty.

For the next half hour, they played hide-and-seek. Nancy found Shelley easily, because she heard Shelley's charm bracelets jingle.

Then Shelley was it. She tagged Bess, who didn't run fast. Bess was it three times in a row. She couldn't find anyone. Everyone got in free while she was looking.

Greg was the best at hiding. He never got caught.

"Let's go inside," Bess complained. "I'm too cold."

"Okay," Nancy agreed.

Nancy and the others ran into the house. The warm air in the kitchen felt good.

"Can we play inside now?" Nancy asked Ann. "It's cold and we're hungry."

"Okay," Ann said. "But you have to

stay out of my way. Why don't you play a game in the living room?"

"We will. Thanks!" Nancy said. Then she sniffed the air. "Mmmm. The pie smells good."

Quickly everyone piled their coats and mittens on a chair in the hall. Then they got out some games and some cards and spread them on the living room floor: Parcheesi and checkers and Go Fish.

When is that pie going to be done? Nancy wondered. She thought she smelled something burning.

Nancy went out to the kitchen. The door was closed. She began to push it open.

But Ann stopped her and stood in the partly open doorway. Her face was red. "What do you want?" she asked sharply.

"We want to make cookies," Nancy said.

"Not now," Ann said. "Come back later."

Nancy was surprised. But she went

back to the living room. They all kept playing games.

After that, Pamela went to see if the pie was done. She was gone for a long time. When she came back, she shook her head. "Not yet," she said.

Then Derrick went. Nancy looked at her watch. It was a quarter past three. "She's still making pie," Derrick announced when he returned. "She wouldn't even let me into the kitchen."

"We'll never get to make cookies," Bess complained.

Finally at four o'clock Hannah came home. Nancy ran to meet her in the kitchen.

"Hannah!" Nancy said. "We've been waiting all afternoon to make cookies!"

"All right," Hannah said. "But I can't think about that now. I need to find something."

"What?" Nancy asked.

Hannah didn't answer. She didn't even take off her coat. She just started looking around the kitchen. She lifted up dishes. She pushed aside canisters.

Frantically, she searched faster and faster.

Nancy thought Hannah looked as if she were going to cry.

"What is it?" Nancy asked. "What are you looking for?"

"My gold ring," Hannah answered. "I left it here on the kitchen counter. And now it's gone!"

2

Snoopy Nancy, Snooty Guest

Your ring is missing?" Nancy asked.

Hannah nodded. She kept looking behind things on the kitchen counter.

Oh, no, Nancy thought. She knew how special that ring was. It was a gold ring with a little diamond in it. It had belonged to Hannah's mother. Hannah always wore it on her right hand. She never took it off except when she was cooking.

"I must have left it here before I went shopping," Hannah said. "And now it's gone!"

"Oh, dear," Ann D'Angelo said.

"That's terrible. Do you want me to help you look?"

Nancy glanced at Ann. All afternoon Ann had been acting strange. Now she looked nervous.

"No. That's all right," Hannah said. "I'm sure it'll turn up somewhere. And you probably need to get home to make dinner for your own family."

"Yes," Ann said, looking at her watch. "It *is* getting late."

Hannah smiled at Ann. "Thanks again for baking that pie. And watching the kids. It was a big help."

"No problem," Ann said.

She began to gather up her things. "This is trash," Ann said, picking up an orange plastic bag that was sitting on the counter. "I'll just put it in the garbage can on my way out." Then she called to Shelley and Greg.

"Have a happy Thanksgiving," Hannah said, trying to sound cheerful.

But Nancy could tell that Hannah wasn't feeling cheerful. She knew Hannah was still very upset.

Oh, dear, Nancy thought. How could this happen? Hannah's gold ring was very precious to her.

Maybe I can help find it, Nancy thought. I'm good at finding things. She hurried to the living room.

"Can we bake cookies now?" Bess asked eagerly.

"No." Nancy shook her head. "I don't think so."

Nancy stared at Pamela and Derrick. They were playing a card game on the floor. They didn't even look up when Nancy came into the room.

"Psst," Nancy whispered to Bess. "Come here."

Bess followed Nancy out into the front hall and around the corner by the stairs.

"Something terrible has happened," Nancy whispered to Bess. "Hannah's gold ring is missing."

"You're kidding!" Bess said. "Did someone take it?"

"I think so," Nancy said.

Quickly Nancy told Bess what had happened.

"Who do you think took it?" Bess asked.

"I don't know," Nancy said. "It could be anyone. Ann D'Angelo was acting kind of funny. And Shelley loves jewelry. But I'll bet it was Pamela. She was in the kitchen a *long* time while we were playing games."

"What about Derrick?" Bess said.

"I don't think so. Ann wouldn't even let him in the kitchen," Nancy said.

"Are you going to make a list in your notebook?" Bess asked.

Nancy smiled. Bess was talking about Nancy's special blue notebook, the one with a pocket. That's where she always wrote down clues when she was trying to solve a mystery.

"Later," Nancy said. "Right now I want to go up to Pamela's room. Maybe Pamela took the ring and hid it up there in her things."

Bess nodded. "Okay. Let's go."

Just then Nancy heard footsteps behind her. She whirled around. Pamela was standing there, scowling at them.

"What is this? Some kind of new American game? I suppose it's called Whispering in the Hall About Your Guests," Pamela said in a snooty tone of voice.

Nancy felt her face turn red. "No," Nancy said. "I was just telling Bess what happened. One of Hannah's rings is missing."

"Oh," Pamela said. "Really? Is that all?"

Nancy's face turned even redder. But this time she wasn't embarrassed. She was angry.

"What do you mean 'Is that all?'" Nancy said. "Hannah's ring is important!"

"Oh, I just meant that *my* nanny is always losing things, too," Pamela said. "And then she finds them a few days later. The ring will turn up. I'm sure of it."

Pamela smoothed the skirt of her green wool dress. "Excuse me," she

said coolly. "I'm going to see if there's anything I can do to help."

With that, she turned and stomped off to the kitchen.

"Whew! What a snob!" Bess said.

Nancy nodded. "See what I mean? She hates us all. And I can't figure out why. I've tried to be nice to her."

Bess shrugged. "Some people are just like that, I guess."

"Anyway," Nancy said, "now's my chance. You guard the stairs. I'm going up to Pamela's room to look around."

"Okay," Bess said. "But hurry."

Nancy quickly peeked in the living room to be sure Derrick wouldn't notice. He was playing a game of solitaire. Then she hurried upstairs and slipped into the first guest bedroom on the right.

Hmmm, Nancy thought. The room was neat and clean. Pamela had made her bed that morning. All her clothes were hung up in the closet. There was nothing much to see.

Nancy tiptoed over to the dresser and

looked on top. She saw a comb and hairbrush, a silver heart necklace on a chain, and two gold barrettes. But no gold ring.

Maybe she hid it in her suitcase, Nancy thought. She glanced at the small navy blue overnight bag. It was sitting on a bench by the window. The top was closed, but it was unzipped.

I could just lift it up and peek inside, Nancy thought, biting her lip.

But Nancy didn't want to do that. She knew it wouldn't be right.

"What do you think you're doing?"

The voice in the doorway startled Nancy. She spun around. Pamela was standing there with her hands on her hips.

"Well!" Pamela said. "This is the most outrageous thing I've ever seen. Do *all* Americans go snooping around in their guests' things?"

3

Caught in
the Act

Nancy's face turned bright red.

"Uh, no," Nancy said. "I mean, I wasn't snooping. I mean, I wasn't snooping in your things."

"Well, what *were* you doing?" Pamela said angrily.

"I was looking for Hannah's ring," Nancy answered.

"In *my* room? So I suppose you think I stole it," Pamela said. She sounded furious.

"N-no," Nancy sputtered. "I mean . . ." Nancy didn't know what to say. She felt so terrible. "I mean, I just thought

I'd look around. Hannah is so upset. I thought maybe she left her ring up here."

Pamela tightened her lips and gave Nancy an angry stare. "Did you look in my suitcase?" she asked.

"No," Nancy said. "Of course not."

"Well, good," Pamela said, calming down. "At least I have *some* privacy."

Nancy blushed. What else could she say? Pamela was right. She shouldn't have snooped.

But I *didn't* look in her things, Nancy thought. Besides, what does she have to hide, anyway? I wonder why she didn't want me to look in her suitcase.

Just then Nancy heard her father's voice downstairs.

"Excuse me," Nancy said. She hurried past Pamela and ran down the front stairs.

Bess was waiting at the bottom, in the same spot where she had been standing guard.

"I'm sorry," Bess said. "She must have gone up the back stairs."

"That's okay," Nancy said.

"Did you find anything?" Bess asked.

Nancy shook her head. "No. But she caught me in her room. Now I guess she *really* hates me."

"Who cares?" Bess said. *"You* don't like *her*. I don't like her, either."

I guess, Nancy thought. But still, she wished that Pamela would be nicer.

A moment later Nancy's father came into the hall. He said hello to Bess and gave Nancy a big hug. Then he told Bess it was time for her to go home.

"But we didn't make cookies yet," Nancy said.

"I know, but it's too late now," Carson Drew said. "It's almost dinnertime. Come on, Bess. I'll give you a ride home."

Nancy went along for the ride in the car. After they dropped Bess off, she told her father what had happened that day.

"Oh, I don't think anyone would steal Hannah's ring," Carson Drew said.

"Hannah probably just left it some-where."

"Like where?" Nancy asked.

"Somewhere around the house," Carson said. "Or maybe she had it on when she went shopping. And then she lost it at the grocery store."

"Well, can we go to the store and look for it?" Nancy asked.

Carson Drew sighed. "We can't search the whole store, Nancy. We have guests at home," he said. "And dinner will be ready soon."

"Oh, please, Daddy?" Nancy begged. "Hannah was *so* unhappy. And I know where to look."

"Where?" Carson asked.

"In the fresh thyme and apples sec-tion," Nancy said. "That's what Han-nah went to buy."

"All right, kiddo," Carson said, giv-ing in.

Carson drove to the supermarket and parked near the entrance. He and Nancy hurried inside. They went right to the fruits and vegetables and looked up and down the aisle.

"Look!" Nancy said. "There it is!"

She saw something shiny mixed in with the parsley and fresh herbs.

"Really?" Carson Drew hurried to look.

Nancy reached into the parsley and pulled out a shiny ring. But it was just a key ring with someone's car keys on it. Her face fell.

"Oh, well," Carson Drew said. "At least it was a nice try,"

Nancy gave the car keys to the store manager. She told him about Hannah's missing ring. He said he would look for it. Then her father drove home.

As Carson Drew pulled into the driveway, he said to Nancy, "Listen, Pudding Pie. I want you to do me a favor."

Pudding Pie was Mr. Drew's special name for Nancy.

"Sure. What is it, Daddy?" Nancy asked.

"Try harder to be nice to Pamela," her father said.

"I'd like to," Nancy said. "But she's not nice to me."

"That's not the point. She's our guest," Carson Drew said. "And her mother told me today that Pamela feels left out. She thinks you don't like her. She thinks you don't want her here for Thanksgiving."

Well, I *don't* want her, if she's going to be so mean, Nancy thought. But she knew her father was right.

"Okay," Nancy said. "I'll try."

But it's not my fault if she won't *let* me be nice to her! Nancy thought.

All through dinner, Nancy tried to talk to Pamela. But Pamela was still angry. She wrinkled her nose at the salmon steaks. She wouldn't eat any salad. She didn't even answer when Nancy asked, "Would you like some cookies for dessert?"

"Cookies?" Derrick said. He looked

puzzled until he saw the plate Nancy was passing him.

"Oh! You mean biscuits," Pamela said. "Yes, I'd love one."

Why does she have to argue with everything? Nancy thought. She can call them biscuits in England if she wants to. Here we call them cookies.

"You'll have to come visit us in London, Nancy," Mr. Morgan said. "We'll treat you to one of *our* best desserts— a nice English trifle."

"What's that?" Nancy asked.

"Oh, it's a lovely layered thing," Mrs. Morgan said. "It has custard and berries and whipped cream and ladyfingers. They're all stacked together in a big glass bowl."

"Sounds yummy. But what are ladyfingers?" Nancy asked.

"They're soft cakes shaped like fingers," Pamela said. "Don't you know anything?"

Nancy sighed. She felt tired. She had been trying hard to get along with Pa-

27

mela all through dinner—but it was no use.

Now she just wanted to go upstairs to be alone. She wanted to think about who took Hannah's ring.

Maybe I can write a list of suspects in my notebook, Nancy thought.

"I'm going to get ready for bed early," Nancy announced when dinner was over.

"Okay," Carson Drew said.

"Don't let the bedbugs bite!" Derrick called. He laughed loudly.

He's just teasing me, Nancy thought. At least he's nicer than his sister.

Nancy climbed the stairs to her bedroom and closed the door. She changed into her favorite nightgown. It was white with a pattern of red and pink roses on it.

Then she walked down the hall to the bathroom to brush her teeth.

"Huh?" Nancy said as she looked at the bathroom sink.

Something was missing. In fact, everything was missing!

"Where's the soap?" Nancy said out loud, even though no one was listening. "And the toothpaste? And my toothbrush!"

Nancy heard someone giggling. Then she heard footsteps. She walked back out into the hall. No one was there.

"Hey," Nancy called. "Is someone up here?"

No answer.

Well, I can't brush my teeth without my toothbrush, Nancy thought. She walked slowly back to her room.

She flipped on the light switch by her door. It was supposed to turn on the lamp by her bed.

But nothing happened. The room stayed dark.

"What's going on here?" Nancy said.

Just then the light in the hallway went out, too.

"Hey!" Nancy cried out.

No one answered.

Nancy was standing all alone—in the dark!

4

Danger
in the Dark

Help!'' Nancy called from the dark hallway.

Silence. No one answered.

Now what? Nancy thought. Was someone going to jump out and shout "Boo!"?

Her heart started to beat a little faster.

It's spooky up here in the dark, Nancy thought. The hall light was always left on at night—even when Hannah and her father were asleep.

"Help!" Nancy called out again.

All at once she heard someone burst

out laughing. It was someone who sounded a lot like Derrick.

"Ha-ha! I got you!" Derrick called as he flipped the hall light back on from the bottom of the stairs.

Then he ran up the stairs to meet Nancy. He had a huge grin on his face.

"Very funny," Nancy said, frowning.

"*I* thought so," Derrick said. He looked totally pleased with himself.

"What's going on?" Carson Drew called from downstairs. "Are you okay, Nancy?"

Nancy ran to the railing and leaned over it.

"*Someone* turned the lights out," Nancy told him. "And the light in my room won't come on, either."

Derrick grinned even more. "Maybe you should try screwing the lightbulb in a little tighter," he said. "I'll bet it's loose."

"So that's what you did!" Nancy said. "You sneaked into my room and unscrewed the bulb while I was in the bathroom."

Derrick just laughed.

"What's going on?" Derrick's mother said. She was standing at the foot of the stairs with Carson Drew.

"Oh, nothing," Derrick answered her.

Julie Morgan walked up the steps. She had shiny red hair and very pale skin. Nancy thought she was pretty.

"Derrick, what have you been up to?" Julie Morgan asked, taking her son by the arm.

But before Derrick could answer, Carson Drew joined them. "Oh, it just sounds like a harmless prank," Nancy's father said quickly.

"Yes, well, when you live with Derrick," Mrs. Morgan said, "you get rather tired of pranks."

She put on a stern face and shook her finger at her son. "Derrick, I want no more of this. Do you understand? No more trouble or I'll send you to bed early."

"Sure," Derrick said, still grinning.

He doesn't even mind being scolded,

Nancy thought as she walked back to her room. He must be used to it.

In the dark, she felt her way to her desk lamp. Then she felt for the bulb. It was loose. She screwed it back in carefully, and the light came on.

Now all I have to do is find the toothpaste and the soap, Nancy thought. I wonder what he did with them?

She went back to the bathroom. The toothpaste and soap were back in their places.

Nancy was glad. She didn't really want to solve the mystery of the missing soap. She wanted to solve the mystery of the missing ring instead. She brushed her teeth and washed her face and went back to her room.

I'm not ready to go to sleep yet anyway, Nancy thought.

She took out her special blue notebook and opened it to a clean page. Then she lay down on her bed. At the top of the page she wrote: "Hannah's Missing Ring."

Then she wrote: "Suspects—Pamela,

Derrick, Shelley, Greg, and Ann D'Angelo."

Under that, she wrote: "What's in Pamela's suitcase?"

Nancy remembered that Pamela didn't want her to look in her suitcase.

What does she have to hide? Nancy wondered. That's what I've got to find out. And soon!

Mmmm. Something smells good, Nancy thought as she woke up the next morning.

Then she remembered. It was Thanksgiving! Hannah was probably already cooking the meal.

She also thought about the missing ring. I've got to find it, Nancy thought. Or Hannah will have a terrible Thanksgiving.

She put on her bathrobe and hurried down to the kitchen.

Pamela and Derrick were already there. They were dressed and eating breakfast at the table. Hannah was at the stove, cooking celery and onions for the turkey stuffing.

"Good morning, Sleepyhead," Hannah said to Nancy with a smile.

"Hi," Derrick said, giving Nancy a big grin. "Want some cereal?" He picked up the box of toasted oat flakes and offered it to Nancy.

"Not yet," Nancy said cheerfully. She ran to the window and looked out. The sun was shining, and it was a beautiful day. "I wonder if the Thanksgiving parade has started on TV yet."

"A parade? For Thanksgiving?" Pamela asked.

"Yes," Nancy said. "It's fun. They have gigantic balloons that look like cartoon characters."

"How silly," Pamela said. "What do balloons have to do with your Pilgrims? Or with giving thanks?"

Nancy's face felt hot. She didn't know what to say. Pamela made fun of everything!

"Oh, it's just a fun way to celebrate,"

Hannah said quickly. "You know, they have Thanksgiving in Canada, too."

"Oh, yes," Nancy said, joining in. "I learned about Canadian Thanksgiving in school."

"So what?" Pamela asked rudely.

"Well, since Canada is like a sister country to England," Nancy said, "I thought maybe the holiday wouldn't seem so strange to you."

Pamela made a face. "You don't say that Canada is a sister to England," she said. "You say it's part of the British Commonwealth."

Then she picked up a raw cranberry from the bowl on the counter. Hannah was using them to make cranberry sauce.

"What are these?" Pamela asked.

"Cranberries," Hannah answered.

Pamela popped it in her mouth and started to chew. "Ew! Disgusting!" she said, spitting it out. "It's sour!"

Nancy sighed and sat down on a kitchen chair.

Is there *anything* she won't complain about? Nancy wondered.

Then Nancy picked up the box of cereal and poured herself a bowl.

"Here—have some milk," Derrick said, handing her the carton.

"Thanks," Nancy said.

At least Derrick is nice to me, she thought.

Nancy opened the top of the milk carton to make the spout. Then she lifted it up and started to pour.

But as soon as she tilted the carton, milk started dribbling out in a fine spray, as if from a watering can.

"Oh, no!" Nancy cried as milk poured all over the table, her bathrobe, and the kitchen floor!

5

Boy Trouble

Ha-ha-ha-ha-ha!" Derrick cried, doubling over with laughter. He had to hold his stomach, he was laughing so hard.

"You creep!" Nancy yelled. She set the milk carton back down. But it was too late. The milk had spilled all over her robe. Even her nightgown had milk on it.

"What's going on?" Hannah asked. She turned around from the stove to see what was happening.

Derrick was laughing too hard to answer. Nancy glared at him, then looked over at Pamela.

Pamela had a worried expression on her face. She looked as if she knew her

brother had done something wrong—
and she didn't think it was funny.

"I have milk all over me," Nancy told
Hannah. "There were holes in the milk
carton and it spilled."

"Oh, my goodness," Hannah said,
grabbing a wet cloth. She started wiping up the spilt milk from the table and
the floor. But there was nothing she
could do for Nancy's bathrobe.

"Derrick, you little twit," Pamela
said. "That wasn't funny when you did
it at home, and it's not funny now. I'm
going to tell Mummy. You'll be sorry!"

"Oh, now, Pamela," Hannah said.
"Don't blame your brother. I don't
think it was his fault."

"Yes, it was," Pamela said. "Look—
he poked tiny holes in the carton, near
the top. That way the milk spills out
all over the place when you pour it. I'm
telling you he's done this before."

She's trying to apologize for her
brother, Nancy thought. She's actually
trying to be nice.

Nancy looked over at Pamela and smiled.

But Pamela didn't smile back. She just got up and walked out of the room.

Fine, Nancy thought. Be that way.

"I'm going upstairs to change," Nancy told Hannah as she got up from the table.

By the time Nancy got back to the kitchen, Derrick's mother was there. Pamela had gone to get her.

"Derrick, I'm very angry with you," Mrs. Morgan said. "These pranks have got to stop!"

"Sorry, Mum," Derrick said. But he still had a small grin on his face.

"We are guests here," Mrs. Morgan went on. "Please act like it and help clean up this mess right away. Then you can spend the rest of the morning in your room—thinking about how other people feel when you play these little jokes of yours."

Derrick bent his head down, hiding his eyes. But Nancy didn't think he looked very sorry.

Well, Nancy thought, at least Pamela

told her mother about it. Maybe she isn't so bad after all. Maybe she didn't steal Hannah's ring.

But who did? That was what Nancy wanted to know.

There were still five people on her list of suspects.

And three of them aren't even here right now, Nancy thought.

"Hannah?" Nancy asked when breakfast was over. "May I walk over to the D'Angelos' house?"

"I guess so. But what for?" Hannah asked.

"I want to talk to Shelley and Greg. To see if they know anything about your ring," Nancy said.

"Nancy Drew, the detective," Hannah said with a smile. But then she looked down at her finger, where the ring should have been. She stopped smiling. "All right," Hannah said. "But don't stay too long. You still have guests here, you know."

Nancy bundled up in her warm jacket and walked the three blocks to the D'Angelo house.

When she got there, she found Shelley and Greg in the living room. They were still in their pajamas. They were sitting on a big couch, watching the Thanksgiving parade on TV. While they watched, they tore up slices of white bread and dropped the pieces into a big roasting pan.

"Hi," Nancy said. Then she looked at the roasting pan. "What are you doing?"

Shelley looked up at Nancy, surprised. "Oh, hi," she said. "We're tearing up bread for stuffing. Want to help?"

"Sure," Nancy said.

"Great!" Greg said. "You can have my place." He jumped up and leaped over a footstool. Then he sat down in another chair.

Nancy laughed and took his place beside Shelley on the couch. "This is fun," Nancy said. She tore up a few pieces of bread and watched the parade.

Then she noticed Shelley's charm bracelets. They were jingling.

Maybe *she* took Hannah's ring, Nancy thought.

"You like jewelry a lot, don't you?" she asked Shelley.

"Not really," Shelley said. "Just charms."

"Oh? How come?" Nancy asked.

"Necklaces look silly on me," Shelley said. "And my mom won't let me pierce my ears. And I hate rings. They make my fingers itch. I just love charms."

Oh, Nancy thought. Then she probably *didn't* take Hannah's ring.

Nancy sniffed the air. She smelled something spicy.

"What's your mom cooking?" Nancy asked.

"Tomato sauce," Shelley answered.

"On Thanksgiving?" Nancy asked. She was surprised.

"Why not?" Shelley said. You can't have lasagna without tomato sauce."

"But are you having turkey, too?" Nancy asked.

"Sure," Shelley said. "Turkey and stuffing and lasagna and salad and antipasto, and everything."

"Oh," Nancy said. She hadn't expected that.

Shelley grinned. "It's an Italian-American Thanksgiving dinner."

Of course, Nancy thought. The D'Angelos are Italian. They eat lots of yummy Italian foods all the time.

"We *always* have lasagna at Thanksgiving," Greg said.

Nancy nodded. "It smells good."

"So why did you come over, anyway?" Shelley asked.

"Oh. I wanted to talk to you about Hannah's gold ring," Nancy said. "I wondered if you saw it or anything."

Shelley and Greg both shook their heads.

"But my mom was talking about it on the way home yesterday," Greg said.

"She was?" Nancy's ears pricked up. "What did she say?"

"She said she thought she remembered seeing it lying on the kitchen counter early in the afternoon, right before she started making pie," Greg said. "Then, later, it was gone."

Nancy looked at Greg. He seemed to be telling the truth. That meant Greg couldn't have taken it. He hadn't gone back to the kitchen after Hannah left.

Okay, Nancy thought. That also proves that Hannah didn't lose her ring at the grocery store or leave it lying around the house. She left it in the kitchen—and someone stole it!

"Well, thanks," Nancy said, quickly tearing up a few more pieces of bread. "That helps me a lot."

Then she put on her jacket and hurried home.

The sun was still shining brightly as Nancy opened her front door.

"I'm home," Nancy called as she went to the coat closet.

No one answered.

Weird, Nancy thought.

"Is anyone here?" she called as she put her hand on the closet doorknob.

But before she could pull it open, it flew open! And something large leaped out at her!

6

The Closet Monster

"**A**rghh!" Nancy screamed as the big dark blue thing came out of the closet toward her.

"Grrrrr! Arghghh!" the blue monster growled.

As Nancy backed up, she saw what it was.

Someone had a coat over his head and was trying to scare her.

"Stop it!" Nancy cried out.

All at once, the monster tossed the coat off his head and started laughing.

"Ah-ha-ha-ha," Derrick cried, doubling over. He pointed at Nancy and started giggling again. "Look at you! You were really scared!"

48

"I was not," Nancy said, putting her hands on her hips. She even smiled.

"I'm sorry," Derrick said. He sounded as if he meant it, although he was still laughing. "I just couldn't resist. I saw you coming up the walk, and I thought, Here's a good chance for a laugh. Don't be angry with me. Please?"

Nancy didn't answer. She wasn't too angry about this prank. But she didn't like his other tricks at all. She was still mad about the milk spilling all over her bathrobe. Now she wouldn't be able to wear it until Hannah washed it.

"Just stay out of the closet," Nancy said. Then she hung her jacket up quickly and ran toward the kitchen without another word.

In the kitchen, Nancy found Hannah basting the turkey. She let Nancy have a turn. It was fun. Nancy liked to squeeze the rubber baster and watch the turkey drippings go up into the glass tube. Then she squirted the juice all over the golden bird.

"How long till dinner?" Nancy asked when they were finished basting.

"Oh, five or six more hours," Hannah said. She put the turkey back in the oven. "We won't eat until five o'clock."

Oh, no! Nancy thought. Six more hours alone with Pamela and Derrick? That didn't sound too good.

Nancy ran to the living room to see if her father could play a game with her. But he was too busy talking to Mr. and Mrs. Morgan.

She hurried back to the kitchen. "May I invite Bess to come over?" Nancy asked Hannah. "To help me keep Pamela and Derrick company," she added quickly.

"Well . . . ," Hannah said slowly. "Okay. As long as you all promise to play together. I don't want you and Bess going off by yourselves all day."

Nancy nodded quickly and hurried to call her friend. But Bess said she could come over for only a little while.

Nancy waited by the front door till

Bess arrived. Then the two of them ran up to Nancy's room.

"We can't stay up here long," Nancy whispered. "We have to play with *them*."

"Did you find the ring yet?" Bess asked.

"No," Nancy said. "And I still don't have any clues. But I went to the D'Angelos' today. Greg said his mom saw the ring on the kitchen counter, so I don't think Hannah lost it."

"Pamela probably took it," Bess said. "She's so nasty."

"I know," Nancy whispered. "She's my first suspect. But I don't have any proof. So all we can do is keep an eye on her."

"Right," Bess agreed. She seemed just as eager to catch the thief as Nancy was.

Then they went downstairs. Carson Drew had made a big fire in the living room fireplace. He set up some board games for them to play on the floor. Then he and the Morgans moved into the den to talk. Nancy and Bess flopped down on the floor.

For a while they played Parcheesi with Pamela and Derrick. Then they played a game called Mazes. Then Nancy's favorite—Clue. Nancy was good at games. She was especially good at Clue. She liked solving mysteries.

After three games of Clue, though, Bess was getting tired. She put her cards on the couch cushions. Then she leaned back.

"It's almost time for me to go," Bess said.

"You can't skip this turn," Derrick said. "That wouldn't be fair."

"Why not?" Bess said.

"Just go on," Derrick said. "Roll the dice. You have to take your turn."

Bess sighed. "I don't even remember what cards I have," Bess said. She reached behind her to the couch, but the cards were gone.

"Look there," Nancy said, pointing. "I think they slipped down between the couch cushions."

Bess put her hands into the crack be-
tween two cushions and dug around.
But she couldn't find all of her cards.
Finally, she lifted one cushion up.

"Hey!" Bess cried, turning around
and smiling at Nancy. "Look what I
just found!"

7

After-Dinner Tricks

Is it the ring?" Nancy cried, leaping up. "Did you find Hannah's ring?"

Nancy rushed over to the couch. She couldn't wait to see what was in Bess's hands.

If it's the ring, Nancy thought, then maybe Pamela took it. She could have hid it in the couch cushions.

"No," Bess said, quickly turning around. "It's just money. A bunch of coins. And look—I even found a fifty-cent piece!"

"Oh." Nancy's shoulders slumped. She was so disappointed.

"May I see?" Derrick said. "I've never seen an American fifty-center."

"Okay," Bess said, handing it over to him.

Just then Carson Drew stuck his head into the room. "What's all the excitement?" he asked. "Did I hear someone say she found Hannah's ring?"

"No, Daddy," Nancy answered. "Bess just found some money in the couch."

"Oh." Carson looked disappointed, too.

I know how you feel, Nancy thought. I wanted it to be the ring.

Then Nancy thought: I've got to hurry if I'm going to catch the thief. The Morgans are going home tomorrow. If I don't catch Pamela by then, she'll leave—taking the ring with her.

Carson Drew got a twinkle in his eye. "Well, finders keepers, Bess," he said. "You may keep the money. Most of it probably fell out of my pockets. So you've won a nice prize for your visit today."

"Really? Gee, thanks," Bess said happily.

Then Carson Drew said it was time

for Bess to go home. Her mother had called. Their Thanksgiving dinner would be ready soon.

"Will we eat soon, too?" Nancy asked. Her stomach was growling.

"Yes," Carson said. "Hannah said the turkey is done early. So why don't you go help her put the food on the table? Everything is just about ready now."

Soon Nancy and her family were sitting down to dinner with their guests.

Nancy was seated between Pamela and Derrick.

"Would you like some cranberry sauce?" Nancy asked as she passed the bowl of sauce.

"Ew," Pamela said. "No, thank you. It's too sour for me."

It's not sour now, Nancy thought. Hannah had cooked the cranberries with sugar. The sauce was sweet.

"Just try some," Julie Morgan said to her daughter. "Take a small bit of each thing."

Nancy piled her plate high with tur-

key, gravy, candied sweet potatoes, cranberry sauce, and stuffing.

But Pamela took only a teaspoonful of each thing. Except for the turkey. She took three big slices of it.

Then she tasted the cranberries.

"Mmmm!" Pamela said. "This *is* delicious. May I have some more, please?"

"Sure," Nancy said as she passed the bowl.

Maybe now she'll like our Thanksgiving more, Nancy hoped.

"I wonder what's for dessert?" Derrick said with a sly grin.

"My goodness. It's too soon to talk about dessert," Derrick's father said. "We haven't eaten dinner yet!"

Derrick laughed. "It's never too soon to talk about dessert," he said.

Nancy glanced at Derrick. He had that sneaky look in his eye.

He's got some kind of prank planned, Nancy thought. I wonder what it is?

Finally dinner was over. Nancy helped clear the table. Then Hannah brought in the pumpkin pie.

"I didn't bake it, so I'm not sure how it came out," Hannah said as she cut slices for everyone.

"Oh, it looks marvelous," Charles Morgan said. "I'm sure we'll love it."

"I'm sure *you'll* love it especially, Hannah," Derrick said with a twinkling smile.

Uh-oh, Nancy thought. Big trouble. He probably poured pepper on the pie while we weren't looking!

Nancy took one bite carefully. "It tastes okay," she said, surprised.

Derrick leaned forward and watched her eat. He stared at Nancy's plate. Then he stared carefully at everyone else. "Eat up!" he said happily.

"Derrick, what are you up to?" Julie Morgan asked her son. "Have you played another one of your very nasty pranks?"

"I'll never tell," Derrick answered mischievously. "But chew your pie carefully, all right?"

Something's going on, Nancy thought. But what?

And why did he say that Hannah would especially like the pie?

Then all of a sudden Nancy thought about Hannah's ring.

"*I* know!" Nancy blurted out. "I'll bet this has something to do with Hannah's ring."

"You guessed it," Derrick said, grinning broadly. "I put it in the pie."

"You what?" Julie Morgan asked. Her mouth dropped open.

"I thought it would be fun to have a bit of our English traditions at this American Thanksgiving," Derrick said.

"Ohhhh," Julie Morgan said. She shook her head, but she smiled, too. Then she turned to Nancy to explain. "You see, at home we always bake small silver rings and prizes in our Christmas steamed puddings. It's for good luck. Whoever gets a prize is supposed to have a whole year of happiness."

"That sounds like fun," Nancy said. "But what's a steamed pudding?"

"It's a dessert made with fruits and bread, baked in a mold," Mrs. Morgan said. "But, Derrick—what did you do?"

"When we were playing hide-and-seek yesterday, I hid in the house," Derrick said.

Nancy's mouth dropped open. So that was it!

"Ann was baking the pie then," Derrick went on. "That's when I saw the ring. So when Ann wasn't looking, I dropped it into the pumpkin pie."

"That was a *terrible* thing to do!" Julie Morgan said.

"It certainly was, young man," Charles Morgan said, shaking his finger at his son. "You've had Hannah worried sick."

"Yes, I was," Hannah admitted. "But let's not fuss. There's no harm done. At least we know where the ring is now. Eat up, everyone!"

Quickly everyone hurried to finish their pie. They chewed each bite carefully, to be sure they didn't swallow the ring. But when the pie was all gone, the ring still hadn't turned up.

"Oh, no," Hannah said. "I can't believe it. My ring is really lost now. I'll never get it back!"

8

Lost—and Found!

But it can't be lost!" Derrick said. "I put it in the pie. I know I did!"

"Well, it's not here now," Carson Drew said. "We've eaten every bite."

"Oh, no," Derrick said. "I'm really sorry. Really I am."

Nancy saw Hannah put a hand up to her cheek. She looked as if she might cry.

"Oh, my," Hannah said. "Do you suppose someone swallowed it?"

"No way," Derrick said. "That was a big ring. And I watched everyone. No one took huge bites. I'm sure you would have chomped on it, if it had been there."

"Then someone stole it from the pie?" Pamela said. Her eyes grew wide.

Maybe, Nancy thought. And maybe not.

"Excuse me," Nancy said, jumping up. "I'll be right back. I want to get my notebook."

Nancy raced up the stairs to her room.

There must be some more clues, Nancy thought. Clues I didn't notice at first and didn't write down!

Think, Nancy told herself. What happened yesterday while Ann was baking the pie?

She sat down at her desk and opened her notebook. Then she started writing everything she could remember.

She wrote:

Got home at 1:00. Ate lunch. Played outside. Hide-and-seek.

Went inside. Pie smelled yummy. Played games.

Went to the kitchen. Was something burning?

4:00—Hannah came home. Ann
left.

Hmmm, Nancy thought. It took Ann
a long time to bake that pie.

Nancy scooped up her notebook and
hurried downstairs.

"Hannah," Nancy said as she
bounced into the living room. "How
long does it take to bake a pumpkin
pie?"

"Oh, about forty-five minutes," Hannah said. "Why?"

"Because I smelled it baking at about
two o'clock," Nancy said. "But Ann
didn't take it out until almost four.
That's long enough to bake two pies."

"Nancy, you're a genius!" Hannah
said. "Do you think Ann baked two
pies and took one of them home with
her?"

"No . . . ," Nancy said slowly, shaking her head. "She didn't take a pie
with her."

"Well, what then?" Carson Drew
asked. He turned and whispered to the

Morgans. "Nancy has solved a number of mysteries around here. She's our own detective."

Then he turned back to Nancy. "Tell us, Pudding Pie. What do you think?"

Nancy smiled. Everyone was watching her. They were all waiting to hear what she would say. Even Pamela.

"I smelled something burning in the afternoon," Nancy said. "I think Ann burned the first pie—so she had to bake another one."

"Ah!" Hannah cried out. She clamped her hand over her mouth. "You're right! I just realized I forgot to tell Ann about our oven. It isn't working right. The temperature is nearly thirty degrees too hot."

Nancy grinned from ear to ear.

"That's why Ann was in the kitchen so long," Nancy said. "And that's why we didn't have time to bake cookies."

"Oh, but it's my fault," Hannah said. "I'm so embarrassed. I should have told her about the oven."

"Just wait right here," Nancy said. She hurried toward the kitchen door.

Nancy opened it and felt a cold blast of air as she stepped outside. But she didn't care. She could hardly wait to look in the garbage can.

She lifted the lid quickly. Near the top, under another bag of garbage, was the orange plastic bag Ann had thrown away when she left the day before. The garbage hadn't been picked up, since it was a holiday.

Nancy lifted the orange bag and brought it into the kitchen. Everyone was waiting for her there. Her cold hands fumbled as she opened the bag.

"Yes! Here it is!" she cried out.

There in the plastic bag was a squished and burned pumpkin pie. Nancy laid the bag open so that Hannah could see. Then she dug her hands into the mushy pie and felt around.

"Can you feel it?" Hannah asked.

Nancy shook her head. She kept pressing her fingers into the mush. Fi-

nally she found it. Something round. And hard like metal.

"Here it is!" Nancy cried, lifting up the pumpkin-covered ring.

"Oh, Nancy, thank you," Hannah said. She grabbed Nancy and gave her a big hug. "I'm so grateful. I don't know what I would have done if I'd lost this ring."

"Any time," Nancy said proudly. She went to wash her hands, smiling so hard that her face hurt.

For a moment Derrick just stood there looking guilty. Then he spoke up.

"Uh, Hannah," Derrick said. "I'm really terribly sorry. I didn't mean it to turn out this way. Honestly."

Hannah stared at him for a moment. Finally she gave him a warm smile and ruffled his coppery red hair.

"Just remember," Hannah said. "Some pranks are funnier than others. I hope you will learn from this how to tell them apart."

After that, everyone went back to the dining room to sit and talk.

Everyone except Nancy. She wanted to be alone for a minute. Then she noticed that Pamela had stayed in the kitchen, too.

"That was amazing," Pamela said. "I mean, how you figured out about the pie. How did you do that?"

"Oh, thanks," Nancy said. "I guess there are *some* things we Americans can do right."

Pamela looked down and blushed. "I'm sorry I've been so mean," she said. "It's just that I didn't know what to do. I didn't know how to act at your Thanksgiving. It's so different. I guess I felt out of place."

Nancy remembered how she had felt that morning at the D'Angelos'. "I know how you feel," Nancy said.

Pamela looked surprised. "You do?"

Nancy nodded.

And I'm sorry I suspected you of taking Hannah's ring, Nancy thought. I guess I wasn't being very nice, either.

"Well, anyway, I hope we can be friends," Pamela said. "I'd love to have an American pen pal. Especially one who's a detective."

"That would be fun," Nancy said. "I've never gotten a letter from anyone in England."

Both girls smiled. Nancy felt so happy. This was turning out to be a great Thanksgiving after all.

"Let's ask Hannah if we can bake cookies tomorrow," Nancy said. "I still want to use my turkey cookie cutter."

"Cookies?" Pamela said. For a minute she sounded puzzled. Then she smiled. "Oh, yes! I like that word. It's much nicer than biscuit."

"I'll say," Nancy said. "I mean, in America, a biscuit is something you eat for breakfast. Unless it's a dog biscuit. Then you feed it to your dog."

Pamela laughed as the two of them walked back to join the others in the dining room. Then, for the rest of the evening, they talked and played in Nancy's room.

But after Pamela went to bed, Nancy

took out her special blue notebook again.

She opened it to the next clean page. At the top she wrote:

Today I solved the case of Hannah's Missing Ring. I also learned that people have all different kinds of holiday traditions. But the nicest holidays are the ones where you try something new—like making a new friend.

Case closed.

FULL HOUSE™
Michelle

#1: THE GREAT PET PROJECT

#2: THE SUPER-DUPER SLEEPOVER PARTY

#3: MY TWO BEST FRIENDS

#4: LUCKY, LUCKY DAY

#5: THE GHOST IN MY CLOSET

Based on the Hit TV Series!

Available from

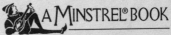

A MINSTREL® BOOK

Published by Pocket Books

Join eight-year old Nancy
and her best friends as they
collect clues and solve mysteries in

THE NANCY DREW NOTEBOOKS™

#1: THE SLUMBER PARTY SECRET
#2: THE LOST LOCKET
#3: THE SECRET SANTA
#4: BAD DAY FOR BALLET
#5: THE SOCCER SHOE CLUE
#6: THE ICE CREAM SCOOP
#7: TROUBLE AT CAMP TREEHOUSE
#8: THE BEST DETECTIVE
#9: THE THANKSGIVING SURPRISE

by Carolyn Keene
Illustrated by Anthony Accardo

A MINSTREL® BOOK

Published by Pocket Books

1045-03